Delectably Wicked Halloween

Jackie Spencer

ISBN: 978-0-615-76668-3

PUBLISHED BY JACKIE SPENCER / CREATESPACE INDEPENDENT PLATFORM /AMAZON

PRINTED IN THE UNITED STATES OF AMERICA

CONTENTS

<u>ACKNOWLEDGEMENTS</u>

Illustrations:

Most illustrations are by Michael Mueller (writer, illustrator and owner of BFB COMIX www.BFBCOMIX.WEBS.COM) Beer for Breakfast, The Coop and Beyond.

Wikipedia is the source used for definition, etymology, history and symbols.

Meet the Crew at Halloween!

Black witches and white witches
Sharing their brew
Werewolves & vampires
With lots of lusty crew
Dark alluring commentary
Just to name a few
Throw in a psycho
That murdered his wife
Then add just a bit
Of sugar and spice,,,,,,,,,,,,
These are the things
That makes up the season
Halloween has great rhyme
Along with good reason

<u>Three Witches</u>

Three witches
Casting their spell
Over the fire
That is hotter than hell

Deep in the woods
Where no one can see
They conjure and cast
Till all is let be

They bring forth the young
To keep their youth
They bring out the blood
To mix with vermouth

Nectar so sweet
No man can resist
Their charms are complete
All three will assist

Fall Spirits Spinning into Your Dreams

Fall is coming
Ghosts are here
Leaves are falling
Much to fear

Hush your mouth
Be very still
The spirits will follow
Your dreams they will fill

In the shadows
Into the night
Spirits fill your dreams
With spooky delight

Some are playful
Some are mean
Some spirits mindful
Spinning into your dream

Definitions of Halloween

The purpose of Halloween was originally to mark the end of summer and the harvest, and the beginning of winter, and to commemorate the passing of the dead.

Halloween or **Hallowe'en** (a contraction of "All Hallows' Evening"), also known as **All Hallows' Eve**, is a yearly celebration observed in a number of countries on October 31, the eve of the Western Christian feast of All Hallows (or All Saints) and the day initiating the triduum of Hallowmas.

According to many scholars, All Hallows' Eve is a Christianized feast originally influenced by western European harvest festivals, and festivals of the dead with possible pagan roots, particularly the Celtic Samhain. Other scholars maintain that it originated independently of Samhain and has solely Christian roots.

Typical festive Halloween activities include trick-or-treating (also known as "guising"), attending costume parties, carving pumpkins into jack-o'-lanterns, lighting bonfires, apple bobbing, visiting haunted attractions, playing pranks, telling scary stories, and watching horror films.

Etymology

The word *Halloween* was first used in the 16th century and represents a <u>Scottish</u> variant of the fuller *All Hallows' Eve* ('evening'), that is, the night before <u>All Hallows' Day</u>. Although the phrase *All Hallows'* is found in <u>Old English</u> (*ealra hālgena mæssedæg*, massday of all saints), *All Hallows' Eve* is itself not seen until 1556.

History

Celtic Influences

Though the origin of the word *Halloween* is Christian, the holiday is commonly thought to have pagan roots. Historian Nicholas Rogers, exploring the origins of Halloween, notes that while "some folklorists have detected its origins in the Roman feast of Pomona, the goddess of fruits and seeds, or in the festival of the dead called Parentalia, it is more typically linked to the Celtic festival of Samhain", which comes from the Old Irish for "summer's end" Samhain (pronounced *SAH-win* or *SOW-in*) was the first and most important of the four quarter days in the medieval Gaelic (Irish, Scottish and Manx) calendar. It was held on or about October 31 – November 1 and kindred festivals were held at the same time of year in other Celtic lands; for example the Brythonic Calan Gaeaf (in Wales), Kalan Gwav (in Cornwall) and Kalan Goañv (in Brittany). Samhain is mentioned in some of the earliest Irish literature and many important events in Irish mythology happen or begin on Samhain. It marked the end of the harvest season and the beginning of winter or the 'darker half' of the year. This was a time for stock-taking and preparing for the cold winter ahead; cattle were brought back down from the summer pastures and livestock were slaughtered. In much of the Gaelic world, bonfires were lit and there were rituals involving them. Some of these rituals hint that they may once have involved human sacrifice. Divination games or rituals were also done at Samhain. Samhain (like Beltane) was seen as a time when the 'door' to the Otherworld opened enough for the souls of the dead, and other beings such as fairies, to come into our world. The souls of the dead were said to revisit their homes on Samhain. Feasts were had, at which the souls of dead kin were beckoned to attend and a place set at the table for them. Lewis Spence described it as a "feast of the dead" and "festival of the fairies". However, harmful spirits and fairies were also thought to be active at Samhain. People took steps to allay or ward-off these harmful spirits/fairies, which is thought to have influenced today's Halloween customs. Before the 20th century, wearing costumes at Samhain was done in parts of Ireland, Mann, the Scottish Highlands and islands, and Wales. Wearing costumes may have originated as a means of disguising oneself from these harmful spirits/fairies, although some suggest that the custom comes from a Christian or Christianized belief (see below). In Ireland, people went about before nightfall collecting for Samhain feasts and sometimes wore costumes while doing so. In the 19th century on Ireland's southern coast, a man dressed as a white mare would lead youth's door-to-door collecting food; by giving them food, the household could expect good fortune from the 'Muck Olla'. In Moray during the 18th century, boys called at each house in their village asking for fuel for the Samhain bonfire. The modern custom of trick-or-treating may have come from these practices. Alternatively, it may come from the Christian custom of souling (see below). Making jack-o'-lanterns at Halloween may also have sprung from Samhain and Celtic beliefs. Turnip lanterns, sometimes with faces carved into them, were made on Samhain in the 19th century in parts of Ireland and the Scottish Highlands. As well as being used to light one's way while outside on Samhain night, they may also have been used to represent the spirits/fairies and/or to protect oneself and one's home from them. Another legend is that a trickster named Jack decided one day to trick the Devil. He trapped the Devil in a pumpkin and paraded him around town. Eventually, Jack let the Devil out and the Devil put a curse on Jack and forever made him a spirit in hell. On Halloween, Jack is released to terrorize the country all night. To protect themselves, the Irish would place a pumpkin with a face outside to scare Jack into believing it was the Devil.

Halloween is also thought to have been influenced by the Christian holy days of All Saints' Day (also known as *All Hallows*, *Hallowmas* or *Hallowtide*) on November 1 and All Souls' Day on November 2. They are a time for honoring the saints and praying for the recently departed who had yet to reach Heaven. All Saints was introduced in the year 609, but was originally celebrated on May 13. In 835, it was switched to November 1 (the same date as Samhain) at the behest of Pope Gregory IV. Some have suggested this was due to Celtic influence, while others suggest it was a Germanic idea.

By the end of the 12th century they had become holy days of obligation across Europe and involved such traditions as ringing bells for the souls in purgatory. "Souling", the custom of baking and sharing soul cakes for "all christened souls", has been suggested as the origin of trick-or-treating. Groups of poor people, often children, would go door-to-door on All Saints/All Souls collecting soul cakes, originally as a means of praying for souls in purgatory. Similar practices for the souls of the dead were found as far south as Italy. Shakespeare mentions the practice in his comedy *The Two Gentlemen of Verona* (1593), when Speed accuses his master of "puling [whimpering or whining] like a beggar at Hallowmas." The custom of wearing costumes has been linked to All Saints/All Souls by Prince Sorie Conteh, who wrote: "It was traditionally believed that the souls of the departed wandered the earth until All Saints' Day, and All Hallows' Eve provided one last chance for the dead to gain vengeance on their enemies before moving to the next world. In order to avoid being recognized by any soul that might be seeking such vengeance, people would don masks or costumes to disguise their identities. In *Halloween: From Pagan Ritual to Party Night*, Nicholas Rogers explained Halloween jack-o'-lanterns as originally being representations of souls in purgatory. In Brittany children would set candles in skulls in graveyards. In Britain, these customs came under attack during the Reformation as Protestants berated purgatory as a "popish" doctrine incompatible with the notion of predestination. The rising popularity of Guy Fawkes Night (5 November) from 1605 onward, saw many Halloween traditions appropriated by that holiday instead, and Halloween's popularity waned in Britain, with the noteworthy exception of Scotland. There and in Ireland, the rebellious Guy Fawkes was not viewed with the same criminality as in England, and they had been celebrating Samhain and Halloween since at least the early Middle Ages, and the Scottish took a more pragmatic approach to Halloween, seeing it as important to the life cycle and rites of passage of communities and thus ensuring its survival in the country.

Spread to North America

North American almanacs of the late 18th and early 19th century give no indication that Halloween was celebrated there. The Puritans of New England, for example, maintained strong opposition to Halloween and it was not until the mass Irish and Scottish immigration during the 19th century that it was brought to North America in earnest. Confined to the immigrant communities during the mid-19th century, it was gradually assimilated into mainstream society and by the first decade of the 20th century it was being celebrated coast to coast by people of all social, racial and religious backgrounds.

Symbols

Development of artifacts and symbols associated with Halloween formed over time. The turnip has traditionally been used in Ireland and Scotland at Halloween, but immigrants to North America used the native pumpkin, which is both much softer and much larger – making it easier to carve than a turnip. Subsequently, the mass marketing of various size pumpkins in autumn, in both the corporate and local markets, has made pumpkins universally available for this purpose. The American tradition of carving pumpkins is recorded in 1837 and was originally associated with harvest time in general, not becoming specifically associated with Halloween until the mid-to-late 19th century.

The modern imagery of Halloween comes from many sources, including national customs, works of Gothic and horror literature (such as the novels *Frankenstein* and *Dracula*) and classic horror films (such as

Frankenstein and *The Mummy*). One of the earliest works on the subject of Halloween is from Scottish poet John Mayne, who, in 1780, made note of pranks at Halloween; *"What fearful' pranks ensue!"*, as well as the supernatural associated with the night, *"Bogies"* (ghosts), influencing Robert Burns' *Halloween* 1785. Elements of the autumn season, such as pumpkins, corn husks and scarecrows, are also prevalent. Homes are often decorated with these types of symbols around Halloween. Halloween imagery includes themes of death, evil, the occult, and mythical monsters. Black, orange, and purple are Halloween's traditional colors.

Trick-or-Treating and Guising

Trick-or-treating is a customary celebration for children on Halloween. Children go in costume from house to house, asking for treats such as candy or sometimes money, with the question, "Trick or treat?" The word "trick" refers to "threat" to perform mischief on the homeowners or their property if no treat is given.

In Scotland and Ireland, guising – children disguised in costume going from door to door for food or coins – is a traditional Halloween custom, and is recorded in Scotland at Halloween in 1895 where masqueraders in disguise carrying lanterns made out of scooped out turnips, visit homes to be rewarded with cakes, fruit and money. The practice of Guising at Halloween in North America is first recorded in 1911, where a newspaper in Kingston, Ontario reported children going "guising" around the neighborhood.

American historian and author Ruth Edna Kelley of Massachusetts wrote the first book length history of

Halloween in the US; *The Book of Hallowe'en* (1919), and references souling in the chapter "Hallowe'en in America": The taste in Hallowe'en festivities now is to study old traditions, and hold a Scotch party, using Burn's poem *Hallowe'en* as a guide; or to go a-souling as the English used. In short, no custom that was once honored at Hallowe'en is out of fashion now. In her book, Kelley touches on customs that arrived from across the Atlantic; "Americans have fostered them, and are making this an occasion something like what it must have been in its best days overseas. All Halloween customs in the United States are borrowed directly or adapted from those of other countries". While the first reference to "guising" in North America occurs in 1911, another reference to ritual begging on Halloween appears, place unknown, in 1915, with a third reference in Chicago in 1920. The earliest known use in print of the term "trick or treat" appears in 1927, from Blackie, Alberta, Canada: Hallowe'en provided an opportunity for real strenuous fun. No real damage was done except to the temper of some who had to hunt for wagon wheels, gates, wagons, barrels, etc., much of which decorated the front street. The youthful tormentors were at back door and front demanding edible plunder by the word "trick or treat" to which the inmates gladly responded and sent the robbers away rejoicing. The thousands of Halloween postcards produced between the turn of the 20th century and the 1920s commonly show children but not trick-or-treating. The editor of a collection of over 3,000 vintage Halloween postcards writes, "There are cards which mention the custom [of trick-or-treating] or show children in costumes at the doors, but as far as we can tell they were printed later than the 1920s and more than likely even the 1930s. Tricksters of various sorts are shown on the early postcards, but not the means of appeasing them". Trick-

or-treating does not seem to have become a widespread practice until the 1930s, with the first U.S. appearances of the term in 1934, and the first use in a national publication occurring in 1939.

Costumes

Halloween costumes are traditionally modeled after supernatural figures such as monsters, ghosts, skeletons, witches, and devils. Over time, in the United States the costume selection extended to include popular characters from fiction, celebrities, and generic archetypes such as ninjas and princesses. Dressing up in costumes and going "guising" was prevalent in Ireland and Scotland at Halloween by the late 19th century. Costuming became popular for Halloween parties in the US in the early 20th century, as often for adults as for children. The first mass-produced Halloween costumes appeared in stores in the 1930s when trick-or-treating was becoming popular in the United States. Halloween costume parties generally fall on or around October 31, often on the Friday or Saturday before Halloween.

Games and Other Activities

ON HALLOWEEN LOOK IN THE GLASS,
YOUR FUTURE HUSBAND'S FACE WILL PASS.

In this Halloween greeting card from 1904, divination is depicted: the young woman looking into a mirror in a darkened room hopes to catch a glimpse of the face of her future husband. There are several games traditionally associated with Halloween parties. One common game is dunking or apple bobbing, which may be called "dooking" in Scotland in which apples float in a tub or a large basin of water and the participants must use their teeth to remove an apple from the basin. The practice is thought by some to have derived from the Roman practices in celebration of Pomona. A variant of dunking involves kneeling on a chair, holding a fork between the teeth and trying to drop the fork into an apple. Another common game involves hanging up syrup-coated scones by strings; these must be eaten without using hands while they remain attached to the string, an activity that inevitably leads to a very sticky face.

Some games traditionally played at Halloween are forms of divination. A traditional Scottish form of divining one's future spouse is to carve an apple in one long strip, then toss the peel over one's shoulder. The peel is believed to land in the shape of the first letter of the future spouse's name. Unmarried women were told that if they sat in a darkened room and gazed into a mirror on Halloween night, the face of their future husband would appear in the mirror. However, if they were destined to die before marriage, a skull would appear. The custom was widespread enough to be commemorated on greeting cards from the late 19th century and early 20th century.

Another game/superstition that was enjoyed in the early 1900s involved walnut shells. People would write fortunes in milk on white paper. After drying, the paper was folded and placed in walnut shells. When the shell was warmed, milk would turn brown therefore the writing would appear on what looked like blank paper. Folks would also play fortune teller. In order to play this game, symbols were cut out of paper and placed on a platter. Someone would enter a dark room and was ordered to put her hand on a piece of ice then lay it on a platter. Her "fortune" would stick to the hand. Paper symbols included: dollar sign-wealth, button-

bachelorhood, thimble-spinsterhood, clothespin-poverty, rice-wedding, umbrella-journey, caldron-trouble, 4-leaf clover- good luck, penny-fortune, ring-early marriage, and key-fame.

The telling of ghost stories and viewing of horror films are common fixtures of Halloween parties. Episodes of television series and Halloween-themed specials (with the specials usually aimed at children) are commonly aired on or before Halloween, while new horror films are often released theatrically before Halloween to take advantage of the atmosphere.

Haunted Attractions

Haunted attractions are entertainment venues designed to thrill and scare patrons. Most attractions are seasonal  Halloween businesses. Origins of these paid scare venues are difficult to pinpoint, but it is generally accepted that they were first commonly used by the Junior Chamber International (Jaycees) for fundraising. They include haunted houses, corn mazes, and hayrides, and the level of sophistication of the effects has risen as the industry has grown. Haunted attractions in the United States bring in an estimate $300–500 million each year, and draw some 400,000 customers, although press sources writing in 2005 speculated that the industry had reached its peak at that time. This maturing and growth within the industry has led to technically more advanced special effects and costuming, comparable with that of Hollywood films.

Treats and Food at Halloween

Because Halloween comes in the wake of the yearly apple harvest, candy apples (known as toffee apples outside North America), caramel or taffy apples are common Halloween treats made by rolling whole apples in a sticky sugar syrup, sometimes followed by rolling them in nuts.

At one time, candy apples were commonly given to children, but the practice rapidly waned in the wake of widespread rumors that some individuals were embedding items like pins and razor blades in the apples in the United States. While there is evidence of such incidents, they are quite rare and have never resulted in serious injury. Nonetheless, many parents assumed that such heinous practices were rampant because of the mass media. At the peak of the hysteria, some hospitals offered free X-rays of children's Halloween hauls in order to find evidence of tampering. Virtually all of the few known candy poisoning incidents involved parents who poisoned their own children's candy. One custom that persists in modern-day Ireland is the baking (or more often nowadays, the purchase) of a barmbrack (Irish: *báirín breac*), which is a light fruitcake, into which a plain ring, a coin and other charms are placed before baking. It is said that those who get a ring will find their true love in the ensuing year. This is similar to the tradition of king cake at the festival of Epiphany.

List of foods associated with Halloween:

- Barmbrack (Ireland)
- Bonfire toffee (Great Britain)

- Candy apples/toffee apples (Great Britain & Ireland)
- Candy corn, candy pumpkins (North America)
- Caramel apples
- Caramel corn
- Colcannon (Ireland)
- Novelty candy shaped like skulls, pumpkins, bats, worms, etc.
- Pumpkin, pumpkin pie, pumpkin bread
- Roasted pumpkin seeds
- Roasted sweet corn
- Soul cakes

Religious Observances

During Hallowmas, many Christian believers visit graveyards in order to place flowers and candles on the graves of their loved ones.

On Hallowe'en (All Hallows' Eve), in Poland, believers are taught to pray out loud as they walk through the forests in order that the souls of the dead might find comfort; in Spain, Christian priests toll their church bells in order to allow their congregants to remember the dead on All Hallows' Eve. The Christian Church traditionally observed Hallowe'en through a vigil "when worshippers would prepare themselves with prayers and fasting prior to the feast day itself." This church service is known as the *Vigil of All Hallows* or the *Vigil of All Saints*; an initiative known as *Night of Light* seeks to further spread the *Vigil of All Hallows* throughout Christendom. After the service, "suitable festivities and entertainments" often follow, as well as a visit to the graveyard or cemetery, where flowers and candles are often placed in preparation for All Hallows' Day.

Perspectives

Christian attitudes towards Halloween are diverse. In the Anglican Church, some dioceses have chosen to emphasize the Christian traditions associated with All Hallow's Eve. Some of these practices include praying, fasting and attending worship services. Father, All-Powerful and Ever-Living God, today we rejoice in the holy men and women of every time and place. May their prayers bring us your forgiveness and love. We ask this through Christ our Lord. Amen. —An All Hallow's Eve Prayer from the Liturgy of the Hours Other Protestant Christians also celebrate All Hallows' Eve as Reformation Day, a day to remember the Protestant Reformation, alongside All Hallow's Eve or independently from it. Often, "Harvest Festivals" or "Reformation Festivals" are held as well, in which children dress up as Bible characters or Reformers. Father Gabriele Amorth, an exorcist in Rome, has said, "If English and American children like to dress up as witches and devils on one night of the year that is not a problem. If it is just a game, there is no harm in that." In more recent years, the Roman Catholic Archdiocese of Boston has organized a "Saint Fest" on Halloween. Similarly, many contemporary Protestant churches view Halloween as a fun event for children, holding events in their churches where children and their parents can dress up, play games, and get candy for free. Many Christians ascribe no negative significance to Halloween, treating it as a fun event devoted to "imaginary spooks" and handing out candy. To these Christians, Halloween holds no threat to the spiritual lives of children: being taught about death and mortality, and the ways of the Celtic ancestors actually being a valuable life lesson and a part of many of their parishioners' heritage. In the Roman Catholic Church, Halloween's Christian connection is sometimes cited, and Halloween celebrations are common in Catholic parochial schools throughout North America and in Ireland. Some Christians feel concerned about the modern celebration of Halloween, and reject it because they feel it trivializes – or celebrates – paganism, the occult, or other practices and cultural phenomena deemed incompatible with their beliefs. A response among some fundamentalist and conservative evangelical churches in recent years has been the use of "Hell houses", themed pamphlets, or comic-style tracts such as those created by Jack T. Chick in order to make use of Halloween's popularity as an opportunity for evangelism. Some consider Halloween to be completely incompatible with the Christian faith, believing it to have originated as a pagan "Festival of the Dead".

Judaism

According to Alfred J. Kolatch in the *Second Jewish Book of Why* Halloween is not technically permitted by Jewish Halakha because it violates Leviticus 18:3 forbidding Jews from partaking in gentile customs. Nevertheless many American Jews celebrate it as a secular holiday, disconnected from its pagan and Christian origins. Reform Rabbi Jeffrey Goldwasser, of the Central Conference of American Rabbis has said that "There is no religious reason why contemporary Jews should not celebrate Halloween as it is commonly observed" while Orthodox Rabbi Michael Broyde has argued against Jews sending their children trick or treating or otherwise observing the holiday. The traditions and importance of Halloween vary greatly among countries that observe it. In Scotland and Ireland, traditional Halloween customs include children dressing up in costume going "guising", holding parties, while other practices in Ireland include lighting bonfires, and having firework displays. Mass transatlantic immigration in the 19th century popularized Halloween in North America, and celebration in the United States and Canada has had a significant impact on how the event is observed in other nations. This larger North American influence, particularly in iconic and commercial elements, has extended to places such as South America, Australia, New Zealand, (most) continental Europe, Japan, and other parts of East Asia.

The Fall Scene

Lovely the fall scene
Haunting our night dream
Bringing us near
Till death lends an ear

Hauntings a must
To love or to lust
Bring forth the fire
That keeps the desire

Halloween season is here
And we all will know fear
And yet we cannot stay away
From the activities we will play

It is a mystery to be shared
We all love to be scared
Our hearts pounding with excite
At the things we do tonight!

Three Little Witches

Three black cauldrons all in a row
One hangs over the fire pit
Swinging to and fro
One is being stirred
By a precocious little witch
The third one is boiling over
With body parts that twitch

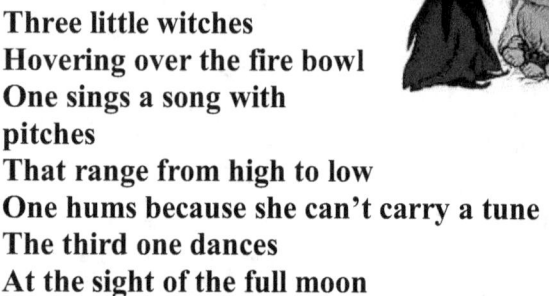

Three little witches
Hovering over the fire bowl
One sings a song with
pitches
That range from high to low
One hums because she can't carry a tune
The third one dances
At the sight of the full moon

Three little witches
Sing and dance away
Along with their broomsticks
Their black cats now do play
Down with the rat tail
That was just laid away
Along with the cat tail
That got caught as a stray

Halloween Moon

Witches cat

With vintage hat

Under the Halloween moon

Black as night

His eyes do fright

Witching hour will come soon

Arched back

Hissing like that

Singing a mournful tune

Black cat spits and spats

Under the light of the moon

Black Cat

Black cat
Witches' hat
In Black basket
Beside black casket

Black cauldron
Cooks the brew
Black cat licks up
Strange stew

Yellow eyes
Share the night
With creatures
Those refer to flight

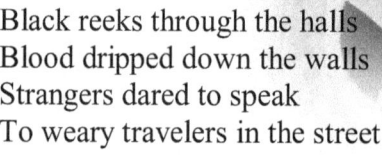

Black reeks through the halls
Blood dripped down the walls
Strangers dared to speak
To weary travelers in the street

Do you hear the spirits calling?
Do you see the night falling?
Black cat steers the way
To see the dead where she lay

Black Casket
Draped in black
Black preacher
Tipped his hat

Black veil hides the tears
Black cat sees your fears
Transformed from a living soul
To wander the earth till debt takes its toll

When the world is wrapped in slumber
And the moon is full in the sky

You can peek out the window

Just to see the witches fly

Excerpt from The Book of Hallowe'en by Ruth Edna Kelley [1919]

Then the flocks were driven in, and men first had leisure after harvest toil. Fires were built as a thanksgiving to Baal for harvest. The old fire on the altar was quenched before the night of October 31st, and the new one made, as were all sacred fires, by friction. It was called "forced-fire." A wheel and a spindle were used: the wheel, the sun symbol, was turned from east to west, sun wise. The sparks were caught in tow, blazed upon the altar, and were passed on to light the hilltop fires. The new fire was given next morning, New Year's Day, by the priests to the people to light their hearths, where all fires had been extinguished. The blessed fire was thought to protect the year through the home it warmed. In Ireland the altar was Tlactga, on the hill of Ward in Meath, where sacrifices, especially black sheep, were burnt in the new fire. From the death struggles and look of the creatures omens for the future year were taken.

The year was over, and the sun's life of a year was done. The Celts thought that at this time the sun fell a victim for six months to the powers of winter darkness. In Egyptian mythology one of the sun-gods, Osiris, was slain at a banquet by his brother Sitou, the god of darkness. On the anniversary of the murder, the first day of winter, no Egyptian would begin any new business for fear of bad luck, since the spirit of evil was then in power.

From the idea that the sun suffered from his enemies on this day grew the association of Samhain with death.

> "The melancholy days are come, the saddest of the year,
> Of wailing winds, and naked woods, and meadows brown and sere.
> Heaped in the hollows of the grove, the withered leaves lie dead;
> They rustle to the eddying gust, and to the rabbit's tread.
> The robin and the wren are flown, and from the shrub the jay
> and from the wood-top call the crow, through all the gloomy day.
>
> "The wind-flower and the violet, they perished long ago,
> And the wild rose and the orchid died amid the summer glow:
> But on the hill the golden-rod, and the aster in the wood,
> And the yellow sun-flower by the brook in autumn beauty stood,
> Till fell the frost from the cold clear heaven, as falls the plague on men,
> And the brightness of their smile was gone from upland, glade, and glen."

--BRYANT: Death of the Flowers.

In the same state as those who are dead, are those who have never lived, dwelling right in the world, but invisible to most mortals at most times. Seers could see them at any time, and if very many were abroad at once others might get a chance to watch them too.

"There is a world in which we dwell,
And yet a world invisible.
And do not think that naught can be
Save only what with eyes ye see:
I tell ye that, this very hour,
Had but your sight a spirit's power,
Ye would be looking, eye to eye,
At a terrific company."

--COXE: Hallowe'en.

These supernatural spirits ruled the dead. There were two classes: the Tuatha De Danann, "the people of the goddess Danu," gods of light and life; and spirits of darkness and evil. The Tuatha had their chief seat on the Isle of Man, in the middle of the Irish Sea, and brought under their power the islands about them. On a Midsummer Day they vanquished the Fir Bolgs and gained most of Ireland, by the battle of Moytura.

"Pumpkins in Patches"

"Scarecrows in corn"

"Lock your Latches"

"Don't open till Morn"

Auspicious Halloween

Halloween baskets

Full of Halloween treats

The sound of children

Playing in the streets

Skipping and jumping all around

Door to door they knock with a sound

Shouting out loud

"Trick or treat"

To some that they follow

Down the dark crowded street

May not turn out to be

So auspiciously sweet

Black Raven Witch

Black Witch
Raven black hair
Black night
Full moon with a glare

Black witch
Eyes black as coal
Heart of black stone
Scars etched on her black soul

Black air
Whispers by
Black stare
You do spy

Black woods where
She can be found
Black ladder-back chair
Where you will be bound

Don't go in the woods
Unless you dare
Black witch
Will take your soul without care

Black Magic

Black Magic it does weave
A tale of tales on Hallows Eve
Black cauldron set on fire,
Tales we will tell to inspire,

Black cat at our heels
Licking up the potion spills,
Take my warning and heed
Don't go in the woods this Hallows Eve

They will catch you and put you
Under their spell,
And your life will be
Like a living hell

Take heart my friends
And don't go there
They will pluck out your eyes
And pull out your hair

Wicked

Wicked thoughts
Wicked words
Wicked nouns
Wicked verbs

Wicked ears
Wicked eyes
Wicked ways
Wicked sighs

Evil Witches

Black hats on witches heads,
Black sheets on their beds,

Black tales of black magic worth looking
Black cauldron with body parts cooking

Into black books of black magic
And black accidents so tragic

Black house with Black light
Black moon with Black night

Black spell that has been cast
Black evil will be at last

It's Hallows' Eve and witches past
Will do their evil at the present task

<u>By The Rusty Garden Gate</u>

Jagged cuts and ragged edges
Sever the flesh of all
Blood can be found on ledges
On every sill and wall

You will try to hide, but can not
It is way too late
You are left here to rot
By the rusty garden gate

The Ghost in the Park

Dressed in white
She waits for her lover
Park bench at night
Her dress bunched under
Where is he?
She began to wonder

One red rose in her hand held tight
Air reeks with the stench of death in the night
As she wanders about in the park unaware
Her life was taken without any care

You can still see her after dark
Sitting there all alone in the park
One red rose in her hand held tight
With the stench of death in the cold dark night

Coaxed from the spirit world

That hovers just above ground

Come now to tell their stories

Victims of untimely deaths found

Lives taken

Dreams shattered

Bruised spirits awaken

Mortal bodies splattered

The End

Black this
Black that
Black coffin
With black mat
Black lace
Black rose
Black silk
Black clothes
Black cat
Black hat
Black cauldron
Black bat
Black parlor
Black ground
Black sky
Black mound
All that is
Is all that was?
Now a memory
Hence, the pause

<u>Steely Eyed Witch</u>

White witch
With white hair
Eyes capture you
With a white glare

One blue eye
The other eye brown
Night captured victims
Buried alive underground

Heed the warning
Must stay clear
Of the steely eyed witch
With the long white hair

Black Witch

Black witch
With raven black skin
Black eyes
Holds coldness within

Black night
That has only one light
The full moon
That shines in the night

Take a chance and travel
Deep in the woods
Be captured by her essence
And tempted with her goods

She will tear you
Limb from limb
Then cook up your body parts
To feed her whim

Your blood will run freely
To the dry black ground
Someone may miss you
Your body will never be found

Ghost in Red

Under the bed
Behind the door
In the attic
Or under the floor

In the basement
In the shed
Where is the ghost
That haunts in red

She wears a red dress
And wears it quite well
She was murdered with spite
And no one could tell

She wants you to find him
That took her life
And cut off his head
Alongside his wife

<u>Under the Porch</u>

Watch out for the seething gory goop

Out of the dirty wooden porch stoop

Its vile filth is rising from under the ground

From which there are bodies buried

Those persons missing,,,,,

,,,, never found

Melancholy Spirit

Melancholy spirit
Lurking the grounds
Haunting the halls
With soft subtle sounds

Searching endlessly for a love
That had been lost
Even searching the gardens
All covered with frost

High and low
Upstairs and down
She whisks with soft flow
Barely making a sound

Floating about slowly
You can catch a glimpse
Feel in the air her presence
As her death was suspense

Murder or suicide
No one really knows
Her body still missing
Found were bloody clothes

Death is but a door

Time is a window

I'll be back

Damned Black Cat

That cat is one hell of a slick cat
Slick as snot
Can get in and out of a mess
When others cannot

Slick as snot
Black as night
Scratches like hell
When in a fight

That damned cat
Has hellish appeal
Street smart ways
He bites at the heel

Eyes in the night
Give off a glow
Won't back down
From any foe

Haunted House on Hill

Lurking in the shadows of time
Was a man dressed so fine
Black suit and black top hat
Vintage apparel along with a tat

A tat which was a name
Of a woman to whom became
A lover so warm and brave
To her charms he became slave

Slave to be destined to live forever
In his distorted views of time
A timely host of many an endeavor
Still lurking in the shadows so fine

Some say it was a spell
That captured their heart
And caused so much terror
For the two to impart

They still haunt the house
That sits upon the hill
And lurk about the property
Every crack and crevice they fill

White Witch (Mocking Lent)

White witch
Eyes of steel blue
Milky white flesh
Eyes that can see through

Hair spun
Of silver and gold
Lovely is she
But her heart icy cold

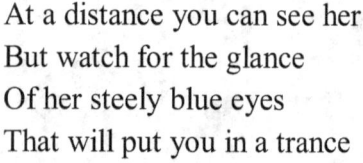

Casts a spell
At the drop of a hat
Stirring up trouble
Along with black cat

At a distance you can see her
But watch for the glance
Of her steely blue eyes
That will put you in a trance

Taking your heart
And blackening your soul
You'll not know what hit you
It is too late to let go

Captured by many
Their souls are spent
She cooks up plenty
To be eaten at lent

<u>Jack O' Lanterns</u>

Jack O' Lanterns burning bright
Looking forward to Halloween night
People stop to gaze at the sight
Small children may engage in a fright

Air is crisp with autumn flair
Burning leaves fill the air
People wondering about town square
Hoping to stir up a really good scare

Spices and herbs you will smell
As cauldrons are brewing up a spell
Casting a bucket into the deep well
In hopes to send evil back to hell

<u>The Vampire</u>

Eyes black and cold

Heart clamped in vice

Cards on table fold

Soul given with a price

No shadow he casts

No reflection is seen

His silent escapades last

Through the night like a dream

Playful Demon Haunting an Inn

About the Inn
He runs lickity split
In and out and back again
And quick as a whip

He is tall and thin
Lanky but stout
With the fairest of skin
Charmed inside and out

Smart though he be
It does not show
Inside his heart
There is a definite glow

A demon of light
No darkness here
His charm is laughter
His soul holds no fear

Demon of light and rules the day
He whisks about as though he were gay
He is curious and lends an ear
Listens in on your conversations so dear

He haunts the Inn where you will stay
And flaunts about like a child at play
He brings the guests gifts and means no harm
This tall wispy character that has so much charm

Husband Ghost

Haunting spirit seeks his love
He searches all night through
Down the halls of the home
He opens doors and windows too

Long ago he lost his wife
She left and was never found
Out of sadness he took his life
Now his spirit walks the ground

Dark Love of the Vampire

This love you have is dark as hell
So dark it makes a tender heart swell
Rich as blood and pepper hot
Longing and yearning as you stir up the plot

Must be flavored with sugar sweet
Hoping to savor your soul as you sleep
From the sweetness of my own lips
Into the dark night as the soul slips

Dark as hell
Dark as night
Dark as the soul
Turns into flight

Feasting on the darkness that draws near
Drinking in the sweetness that most fear
Blood rich and satisfyingly warm
Dark love that only means you most harm

<u>Book & Candle</u>

Book with spell
To heal the mind
Meditation & prayer
A must to unwind
Candle lit
Favor to ask
Love is the answer
To any task

Betrayed Witch

Cold black stare
From her deep green eyes
And a disturbing glare
To the one she does despise

Death will come soon
From not far behind
A slow agonizing doom
Your bones she will grind

You should have known
To not have betrayed
For soon now your bones
Will be turning in your grave

You get what you deserve
She chants as she makes you blind
Her deep green eyes blurred
By her twisted vengeful mind

Torture you she will
It is her vengeful way
Your betrayal is still
On her mind to this day

Black cloud of smoke
Will cover the sky
As her spells you will choke
In the cage where you lie

The cage is ragged
And full of rust
Just as your mind
Fills with disgust

You're choking
You're blind
Your bones
She will grind

Then what is left
Will be buried in the ground
She will dance on your grave
Her happiness not so profound

Her vengeance now deemed
She has declared her pain
To be whisked squeaky clean
In the cold, dark, rain

Zombies

It's Hallows eve
All will chant
Trick or treat?
As the undead rant

Zombies by the dozens
Come out to feast
On living flesh
To say the least

They will eat the children
That couldn't get away
And the undead linger
To wander another day

Gothic Gate
Apple Crate
Sinister Look
Black Spell Book

Jack O Lantern Lit
Black Candle Wick
Black Crow
Dreadful Foe

Vengeful Spirit

In the darkness of her room
There is more than just gloom
Enters now a different air
Sitting in her favorite chair

The air speaks with a muffled sound
The words seem to come from under ground
Spirit full of suffering and pain
Whispers over and over again her name

She tries to communicate without fear
The spirit is becoming more clear
As to whom she is and what she wants
For in this particular room she haunts

It was here where her life
Was taken away
Murdered by a lover
Now he must pay

Take his life and end it well
Send his mortal remains to hell
Take his life like he took mine
My soul will linger on in time

Dagger in and thrust it deep
Don't kill him now in his sleep
Take his life when he can see
Seeing the pain will satisfy me

A Dream of Death

Broken shell
Windswept spell
Under water scene
Calm and serene

Sparkling sand
Magical dream
Swaying frond
Pleasingly green

Silent wave
Sweeps over me
Into grave
No sky I see

Gazing into wonder
My eyes do see
The infinite dream
That is meant for me

Turning over and over
In my own mind
As I ate my last apple
And drank my last wine

<u>Zombie Spell</u>

Conjuring up
A spell so cold
Out of the book
Of spells unfold
Worn pages
And ages old
Its spine is weak
But will still hold
All the pages intact
And can still be read
A spell to procure
The living from the dead

Vengeful White Witch

White witch roaming the grounds
Outside of coffin she can be found

Once in love but it didn't last
Even in death she thinks of the past

Reeking vengeance black as sin
Haunting the one who wouldn't give in

Tormenting his life until he is dead
He'll be buried beside her in a coffin of dread

<u>White Witch, Black Witch</u>

White witch, Black witch
In the woods with black pitch
Black cauldrons all afire
Blazing madness with their desire

White witch, black witch
Having lots of fun
Conjuring spells with a hitch
That speaks loudly as a pun

White witch, black witch
With their poetic black spell
Cut out the tongue of the snitch
That betrayed them all to hell

Halloween's a Coming

Halloween's a coming
It is loud and clear
We will go a haunting
You and I, my dear

Halloween's a coming
And it won't be long
We will be hopping and skipping
Singing a Halloween song

Breezes blowing
Cool autumn air
Apples being picked
To make candy for the fair

Scarecrow in the corn field
To scare away the crows
Corn must be harvested
Before the winter snows

We will put on our costumes
And pack a bag for treats
We will go door to door
And ask for tricks or sweets

Halloween's a coming
And you can be sure
That it will be lots of fun
As the night becomes more obscure

Scaredy Cats

Three little black cats
On Halloween night
Went out to trick or treat
And intended not to fright

Three little black cats
All in a row
Hissing and scratching
As they met with a foe

She tried to capture them
And put them in her sack
They screamed and cried
As they hunched up their back

She was tall and lanky
With a long thin nose
Long white hair
Wearing all black clothes

She cackled out loud
When she heard them scream
It tickled her fancy
To fulfill her wildest dream

Capturing three little black cats
To cook in a stew
Would make her a potion
A black magic brew

Three little black cats
Did get away
And the white haired witch
Will have a debt to pay

Three little black cats
So scared now, they will bite
No more trick or' treating for them
On Halloween night!

<u>Cruel White Witch</u>

White witch
White witch
Why are you
So cruel?

Spells cast
In distant past
Up now
For renewal

For in a witches mind
Never to forget the past
Betrayal not kind
In memories that last

Fire burns bright
Under the cauldron so black
Conjured up spirits
To prepare a flask

A flask to carry
A potion so pure
Not even the strongest
Mind can procure

The flask is made
Of silver and gold
It mesmerizes even
The strongest and bold

"Salem Witches Brew"
A Recipe

Eye of Newt
Toe of Frog
Wing of bat
Tongue of dog

Adders Bark
Blind worm's sting
Lizard's legs
Howler's wing

For a charm
Of powerful trouble
Like a hell broth
Boil and bubble

Salem Mass 1689

Hallows Eve

Tell me the story of old Hallows Eve
How witches, werewolves & vampires would heave
A bevy of excitement over the land
Havoc and terror would be dancing to the band
There would be mist-filled valleys, and moors spread
with fog
Creatures so frightening coming out of the bog
Haunted houses with ghosts doing dastardly deeds
Conjured up spirits that the devil has conceived
Making your house and the walls bleed
All in the good old days of Old Hallows Eve.

__Witches Tears__

Witches Hat
Witches Brew
Witches Rat
Witches Shoe

Witches Heart
Witches Ears
Witches Eyes
Witches Tears

All who sees
All who knows
Witches heart
Is all aglow

Hardened by life
Insults and pain
Hardened by betrayals
More losses than gain

Witches heart
Witches fears
Witches eyes
Filled with tears

Red Witch

This Poem written by Michael Mueller

ON HALLOWEEN NIGHT
RED WITCH CASTS A SPELL
SHE'LL TORMENT HER LOVER
THEN SEND HIM TO HELL
SHE CONJURED HER SPIRITS
AND BLINDED HIS EYES
MADE HIM A SLAVE
TO HER WILL AND HER LIES

SHE PULLED OUT HIS HEART
AND HELD IN HER HAND
THE POWER TO USE AND
MANIPULATE MAN
BLOODTHIRST INSATIABLE
SHE DRAINED IT DRY
THEN HANDED IT BACK TO HIM
AND SAID GOODBYE

SORROW DESCENDED
BUT DIDN'T LAST LONG
IT SOON TURNED TO HATRED
HE FELT IT SO STRONG
EVIL RED WITCH
WILL STILL HAVE HER DAY
EVEN IN HELL
WHERE HER LOVER WAITS...

Ugly Old Witch

She was an ugly old witch
With a long crooked nose
With long crooked fingers
And long crooked toes

Her complexion is hideous
And takes a shade of green
It has bumps, zits and knots
The rest remain to be seen

Her hair is long in length
That goes past her large but
She has long skinny legs
And a very large gut

She is unkempt and unclean
Her breath smells like poop
She has dirty long fingernails
From scratching the stoop

She lives in the woods
Not far from your home
On Halloween night
Don't leave children alone

For it is then when her power
Becomes more potent and strong
Specially in the twilight hour
All Halloween night long

Tormented Ghost

In the archives of my mind
I will search and I will find
The invitation I need
Allowing me to proceed

All the avenues of pain
Those are related to the brain
Takes on a masterful deception
Conquering love's legible reception

When darkness falls
And moon takes its place
The light that reflects
Will shine on your face

I will see you for what you are
And not who you pretend to be
I will know in my heart
The search will be over for me

The spell that I cast
Will forever be
In death it will last
For all here to see

To wander after death
Searching all night long
Constant agony I feel
As I sing a soft,,,
         Sweet,,,
            Song,,,,,,,,,,,,

Ghost from the Pier

He is vile and filthy
With dirty long hair
He speaks with twisted tongue
And stinks up the air

You will know he is near
When you smell death
This ghost from the pier
Is full of wickedness

He is cursed to walk
The rotten filthy pier
And is destined to stalk
The living that comes near

The ghost has a name
That is frightening to say
He had much fame
Once upon a time in his day

He was famous
And once was kind
Then through love
His heart strings did bind

It was love
That took him away
Turning to hate
On this cold winters day

Betrayals were many
With his lusty mate
She was a cold hearted woman
With no love for her fate

He couldn't get over this feeling
His mind did portray
Fathomless pits of betrayals reeling
Over and over in his mind as he lay

On the pier near the village
He took his own life
Could not take any more
Of heartbreak from his wife

He wanders around all the night through
Pondering about what more he could do
He speaks unsteadily mumbling about
His mind is so twisted that nothing comes out

You can catch a reflection
In the water off the pier
He is standing behind you
Your heart feels the fear

He comes near dusk
To haunt the pier
Where once in lust
He married her here

<u>Three Little Witches Trick or Treating</u>

Three little witches
Wearing colorful britches
Colors of orange and green

Hats on their heads
And boots on their feet
They will celebrate Halloween

Carrying their brooms
Black cats at their sides
Bags in hands for their treats

From door to door
They shout out for more
"Tricks or please for some sweets"

Cute Little Witch Casts a Love Spell

Crooked broom
A magical loom
And a cute little witch
That she be

Cooked up a brew
Called it a stew
Hot and bubbly
Serving dinner for me

Frogs legs
Spiders' eggs
My dreams
To come true

Spell cast
Love at last
Delectable spirit
In you

<u>CSI</u>

It was horrendously vulgar
I was squeamish at the site
Signs of torture were prominent
Half eaten corpse smelled ripe

Flesh torn and eaten ravenously
Drained of blood rich and red
Now drenched and stained boldly
Once white sheets on four poster bed

The love of fresh blood and flesh
Were signs of a savage mind
Along with course hair and fiber
Mushy gooey substance left behind

Course hair of animal nature
Fiber from ragged aged cloth torn
Was found near the horror scene
Long stem red rose with one thorn

One prick of this beauty
With forbidden treasure
Short lived excitement
Ended in bloody pleasure

A Mother Spirit Searching for Lost Child

Alone in the attic
She was looking to see
If someone was searching
Or looking for me

Sheltered by a storm
Alone in the night
In the attic room dark
Not near enough light

A rocking chair found
And was covered in dust
She will sit quietly
And think in disgust

Rocking and swaying
Back and forth
Creaking and squeaking
Across on the floor

Seeing what only
She can see
Looking and searching
For a lost lonely me

Her spirit is still there
In the attic all night
Rocking in that chair
Till morning's first light

Chaotic Ghosts

Ghosts in the garden
Roaming the ground
Ghosts in the home
Where you will be found

Ghosts in the woods
Near the ocean at night
Ghosts of the dead
Those come out to fright

Spirits still haunting
This old house as it were
Left alone and still wanting
At last to be heard

Death came too sudden
Life very short
Murder and suicide
Of chaotic distort

Jack O' Lantern

Overtures of sharp pain
Flickering with the light
Come out to haunt the living
As day fades away into night

Jack O' Lantern comes to life
When it is fully lit
On Halloween night
No longer will it wearily sit

He will walk amongst the living
Till the one he wants is dead
He will take his life giving
Slashing off his stupid head

Book of Dark Shadows

Spells cast
From humble past
Book of dark shadows will be

Pages are worn
Binding is torn
All is still worthy for thee

Written spells
From aged veils
Are sure to last for free

Safety and power
In the Witching Hour
Are revealed for all to see

Three Little Witches That Lost Their Britches

Three little witches
Lost their britches
They began to sigh

Oh mother
We regret to say
We have lost our britches

Lost your britches
You naughty witches
Now you cannot fly

On hallows eve night
When all will fright
You will be grounded

Grounded witches
That lost their britches
This is a funny sight

Now they will dance
Without any pants
All in the full moon light

Kitchen Witch Recipes

*In the next few pages
we share with you some special recipes from our
kitchen.

A Charm for Protection When Traveling

With your mortar and pestle, grind together 1 tsp. Rosemary and ½ tsp. Patchouli while meditating on safe travels.
Knead your herbs into a handful of no-bake clay.
Flatten the clay until it is no more than ½ inch thick.
Carve symbols of protection (Triquetra and Eye of Horus)
Directly onto the clay with a pointy object.
Set aside and grab your stone of Jade.
With your Jade in your dominant hand, charge it with intentions of safe travel and focus on your journey free from obstacles.
Press your charged stone into the center of your clay. (If you feel that it may come loose, adhere it with a few drops of glue.)
Place your amulet between two purple candles.

Light the candles and enchant the following:

As I travel and venture about
Regardless of my choice in route
I ask for protection be it visible or unseen
With no mishaps, please intervene
By herb, stone and clay of protection
Return me safely home in complete perfection.

Allow clay to dry.
Store it in a purple cloth bag and carry it on you or punch a small hole in the top to hang it within your vehicle.

To Banish Negative Forces in Your Home

To banish negative forces or negative energies in your home:

One whole onion: cut in quarters.
Place a quarter in each corner of your room overnight. The next day, wearing rubber or plastic gloves, chop them up and bury them in the ground.

Do this for 7 days in a row.

Spell to Enchant Words Written

This spell is used to write successful letters for either a love interest or for business.

Take a piece of stationery and rub all over it with lavender.

Write with crimson ink (known as Dove's Blood)

Whatever the letter is meant to read, the person who has written the letter will be granted their wishes.

Enabling Your Heart's Desire (Love Spell)

Take a sachet bag containing sage, rosemary and thyme.
Keep in a drawer or under a pillow or for better results wear it against the skin.

The bag must be moistened every *seven* days with *seven* drops of bergamot oil to be truly effective in enabling your heart's desire.

Meditation and prayer are of strategic importance for spells to work. "Be specific for what you ask for"

Forever Friends

To ensure friendship to last forever:

Take two little bags and place whole cloves in each then sew up the bags (preferably by hand).
One being carried at all times by each of the friends concerned.

Simple herbal bag to protect children from nightmares.
A bit of muslin or a cotton tea bag. Fill the bag with
thyme, hops flowers, and rosemary.
Pray over the bag. Pin the bag inside
the child's pillow case. Say aloud,
'let nightmares plague my
children no more.

For Lovers' Sweet Dreams

Place a handful of red rose petals, a handful honeysuckle flowers, and one tsp. of powdered orris root, one xcixnti. of allspice, and a lock of the spell maker's hair in a small bag made of muslin. Seal the bag by sewing it up by hand. The bag then must be moistened thoroughly with pine oil.

When you place this under your pillow the person you wish for should dream only dreams of you.

Healing Spell

Healing thoughts sent to flight
Bring the brightest of blessings
This very night
Send this healing white light from above,
Surround my friend now
 in healing love.

Herbs & Spices

In the next several pages are a list of some herbs and spices, their definitions and uses that we want to share with our readers.

An Explanation of Medicinal Plants

The vegetable world comprises three main groups of plants: Superior, Intermediary and Inferior. These encompass bacteria, microscopic algae, mushrooms, ferns, brushes and trees. Their identification is a task of specialists and the limit between the vegetal and animal world is not clear. To simplify matters, we consider plants those recognized as such by ordinary people. Herbs are seed producing annual, biennial or perennial plants that do not develop a persistent woody tissue. Because herbs have such an important historical and tradition value in healing, sometimes they are treated as a special category of plants. Herbs are particularly valued for their medicinal, savory or aromatic qualities. In the following list, herbs are considered as medicinal plants and taken only for their medicinal or aromatic properties.

1)ALOE VERA: *Aloe vera syn. A. barbadensis* (Liliaceae)

HISTORY and USES

Native to Africa, *aloe vera* is commonly cultivated elsewhere. The clear gel found inside the plant's leaf and the crystalline part found alongside the leaf blade, which contains *aloin*, are both used for medicinal and cosmetic purposes. The clear gel is a remarkably effective healer of wounds and burns, speeding up the rate of healing and reducing the risk of infection. The brownish part containing *aloin* is a strong laxative, useful for short-term constipation. Aloe is present in many cosmetic's formulae because its emollient and scar preventing properties.

MAIN PROPERTIES: Heals wounds, emollient, laxative.

2) ANGELICA

Angelica arcangelica (Umbelliferae)

HISTORY and USES

Angelica has a long-standing record as a prized medicinal herb and has been mentioned by European herbalist since the 15th Century. Angelica has been used to reduce muscular spasms in asthma and bronchitis. It has also been shown to ease rheumatic inflammation, to regulate menstrual flow and as an appetite stimulant. The stems are candied for culinary use.

MAIN PROPERTIES: Antispasmodic, promotes menstrual flow.

3) ANISE

Pimpinella anisum (Umbelliferae)

HISTORY and USES

Anise has been cultivated in Egypt and known to the Greeks, Romans and Arabs, who named the plant *anysun*. Since Antiquity it has been used as a flavoring spice in recipes and as a diuretic, to treat digestive problems and to relieve toothache. Anise seeds are known for their ability to reduce flatulence and colic, and to settle the digestion. They are commonly given to infants and children to relieve colic, and to people of all ages to ease nausea and indigestion. It also has an expectorant and antispasmodics action that is helpful in countering period pain, asthma, whooping cough and bronchitis. The mild hormonal action of anise seeds may explain its ability to increase breast-milk production and its reputation for easing childbirth and treating impotence and frigidity. Anise essential oil is used externally to treat lice and scabies

MAIN PROPERTIES: Reduces colic and flatulence, promotes digestion, antispasmodic

4) ARNICA: *Arnica civnti-in* (Compositae)
HISTORY and USES

Arnica has been used extensively in European folk medicine. The German philosopher and poet Goethe (1749-1832), claimed arnica for ease his angina in old age. Herbalism and homeopathy use arnica extracts, ointments and compresses to reduce inflammation and pain from bruises, sprains, tendons, dislocations and swollen areas. Arnica improves the local blood supply and accelerates healing. It is anti-inflammatory and increases the rate of reabsorption of internal bleeding. The internal use of arnica is restricted to homeopathic dosages as it is potentially toxic.

MAIN PROPERTIES: Anti-inflammatory, germicide, muscular soreness, pain relieving.

5) BASIL, HOLY BASIL
Ocimum sanctum (Labiatae)
HISTORY and USES

Holy basil, like sweet (culinary) basil, comes from India where it is revered as a sacred herb. The Egyptians burned a mixture of basil and myrrh to appease their gods. Sweet Basil (*Ocimum basilicum*) was introduced in Europe as a seasoning for food. The herb has very important medicinal properties – notably its ability to reduce
blood sugar levels. It also prevents peptic ulcers and other stress related conditions like hypertension, colitis and asthma. Basil is also used to treat cold and reduce fever, congestion and joint pain. Due to its anti-bacterial and fungicide action, basil leaves are used on itching skin, insect biting and skin affections.

MAIN PROPERTIES: Lowers blood sugar levels, antispasmodic, analgesic, lowers blood pressure, reduces fever, fungicidal, anti-inflammatory.

6) BELLADONA, DEADLY NIGHTSHADE

Atropa belladonna (Solanaceae)

HISTORY and USES

Deadly nightshade is native to Europe, western Asia and northern Africa. *Herba bella dona*, or "herb of the beautiful lady" is known for its poisonous effects (belladonna increases heartbeat and can lead to death), like many other plants it is an important and beneficial remedy when used correctly. Belladonna contains *atropine* used in conventional medicine to dilate the pupils for eye examinations and as an anesthetic. In herbal medicine, deadly nightshade is mainly prescribed to relieve intestinal colic, to treat peptic ulcers and to relax distended organs, especially the stomach and intestine. Deadly nightshade is also used as an anesthetic in conventional medicine.

MAIN PROPERTIES: Smooth muscle, antispasmodic, narcotic, reduces sweating, sedative.

7) BENZOIN GUM
Styrax benzoin (Styraceae)
HISTORY and USES
Benzoin is a tree native to South-East Asia. Its trunk exudes a gum well known for its strong astringent and antiseptic action. For this reason it is used externally to fight tissue inflammation and disinfection of wounds. When taken internally, benzoin gum acts to settle griping pain, to stimulate coughing, and to disinfect the urinary tract. Benzoin gum is widely used in cosmetics as an antioxidant in oils, as a fixative in perfumes and as an additive to soaps. When steam inhaled, it helps healing sore throats, head and chest colds, asthma and bronchitis.
MAIN PROPERTIES: Antiseptic, astringent, anti-inflammatory.

8) BERGAMOT
Citrus bergamia syn. C. aurantium var. bergamia (Rutaceae)
HISTORY and USES
Bergamot oil, expressed from the peel, assists in avoiding infectious diseases. In cosmetics it is used in preventing oily skin, acne, psoriasis and acne. The oil (or constituents of it) is sometimes added to sun-tanning oils. Bergamot oil is also used to relieve tension, relax muscle spasms and improve digestion.
MAIN PROPERTIES: Disinfectant, muscle relaxant.

9) BITTER ORANGE
Citrus aurantium (Rutaceae)
HISTORY and USES
The bitter orange, native to tropical Asia, has provided food and medicine for thousands of years. Its oil contains *flavonoid*s which are anti-inflammatory, antibacterial and antifungal. Bitter orange juice is rich in

vitamin C which helps the immune system. As an infusion, it helps to relieve fever, soothe headaches and lower fever. It yields *neroli* oil from its flowers, and the oil known as *petitgrain* from its leaves and young shoots. Both distillates are used extensively in perfumery. Orange flower water is a byproduct of distillation and is used in perfumery and for flavoring. Reduces heart rate and palpitations, to encourage sleep and calm the digestive tract.

MAIN PROPERTIES: Anti-inflammatory, antifungal, antibacterial, digestive.

10) CALENDULA, MARIGOLD
Calendula officinallis (Compositae)
HISTORY and USES

Marigold is one of the best herbs for treating local skin problems. Infusions or decoctions of Calendula petals decrease the inflammation of sprains, stings, varicose veins and other swellings and also soothes burns, sunburns, rashes and skin irritations. These remedies are excellent for inflamed and bruised skin, their antiseptic and healing properties helping to prevent the spread of infection and accelerate the healing. Marigold is also a cleansing and detoxifying herb, and the infusion and tincture are used to treat chronic infections. Taken internally, it has been used traditionally to promote the draining of swollen lymph glands such as tonsillitis.

MAIN PROPERTIES: Anti-inflammatory, astringent, heals wounds, antiseptic, detoxifying.

(11) CAMPHOR
Cinnamomum camphora syn. Laurus camphora (Lauraceae)
HISTORY and USES

Camphor trees are native to China and Japan and are cultivated for its wood for the extraction of camphor oil.

Marco Polo was the first to note that the Chinese used camphor oil as a medicine, scent and embalming fluid. Camphor crystals have strong antiseptic, stimulant and antispasmodic properties and are applied externally as unguents or balms as a counter-irritant and analgesic liniment to relieve arthritic and rheumatic pains, neuralgia and back pain. It may also be applied to skin problems, such as cold sores and used as a chest rub for bronchitis and other chest infections.

MAIN PROPERTIES: Antiseptic, antispasmodic, analgesic, expectorant.

12) CARDAMOM
Elettaria cardamomum (Zingiberaceae)
HISTORY and USES
Cardamom has been praised as a spice and medicine and used in ancient Egypt to make perfumes. It is an excellent remedy for many digestive problems, helping to soothe indigestion, dyspepsia, colon spasms and flatulence. It has an aromatic and pungent taste and combines well with other herbs and helps to disguise the less pleasant taste of other herbs.

MAIN PROPERTIES: Eases stomach pain, carminative, aromatic, antispasmodic.

13) CELERY, SMALLAGE
Apium graveolens (Umbelliferae)
HISTORY and USES
More familiar as a vegetable than as a medicine, celery finds its main use in the treatment of rheumatism, arthritis and gout. Containing *apiol*, the seeds are also used as a urinary antiseptic. Celery is a good cleansing, diuretic herb, and the seeds are used specifically for arthritic complaints where there is an accumulation of waste products. The seeds also have a reputation as a

carminative with a mild tranquilizing effect. The stems are less significant medicinally.

MAIN PROPERTIES: Anti-rheumatic, antispasmodic, diuretic, urinary antiseptic.

14) CHAMOMILE, GERMAN CHAMOMILE

Chamomilla recutita syn. Matricaria recutita (Compositae)

HISTORY and USES

Chamomile grows wild in Europe and west Asia. Related species are found in North America and Africa. Its flowers help to ease indigestion, nervousness, depressions and headaches, being ideal for emotion related problems such as peptic ulcers, colitis, spastic colon and nervous indigestion. Chamomile's essential oil have anti-inflammatory, anti-spasmodic and anti-microbial activity. It is an excellent herb for many digestive disorders and for nervous tension and irritability. Externally, it is used for sore skin and eczema.

MAIN PROPERTIES: Anti-inflammatory, antispasmodic, relaxant, carminative, bitter, nervine.

15) CHICORY

Cicorium intybus (Compositae)

HISTORY and USES

Chicory is native to Europe and have been cultivated through the ages. As a tea or extract, chicory root is a bitter digestive tonic that also increases bile flow and decrease inflammation. Its roasted root is commonly used as a coffee substitute. Chicory is an excellent mild bitter tonic for the liver and digestive tract. The root is therapeutically similar to dandelion root supporting the action of the stomach and liver and cleansing the urinary tract. Chicory is also taken for rheumatic conditions and gout, and as a mild laxative, one particularly appropriate for children. An infusion of the leaves and flowers also aids the digestion.

MAIN PROPERTIES: Digestive, liver tonic, anti-rheumatic, mild laxative.

16) CINNAMON

Cinnamomum verum syn. C. zeylanicum (Lauraceae)

HISTORY and USES

Cinnamon is native to Sri Lanka, growing in tropical forest and being extensively cultivated throughout the tropical regions of the world. Cinnamon has a long history of use in India and was first used medicinally in Egypt and parts of Europe from about 500 BC. The infusion or powder is used for stomach pains and cramps. Traditionally, the herb was taken for colds, flu and digestive problems, and it is still used in much the same way today.

MAIN PROPERTIES: Warming stimulant, carminative, and antispasmodic, antiseptic, anti-viral.

17) CLOVE

Eugenia caryophyllata syn. Syzgium aromaticum (Myrtaceae)

HISTORY and USES

Clove trees are original from Indonesia. The dried flower buds, clove, are extensively used as spice. The buds, leaves and stems are used for the extractions of clove's oil. Both the oil and the flower buds have been valued as a herbal medicine for a long time. The oil contains *eugenol*, a strong anesthetic and antiseptic substance. Cloves are also well known for their antispasmodic and stimulating properties.

MAIN PROPERTIES: Antiseptic, mind and body stimulant, analgesic, antibacterial, carminative.

18) COMFREY, KNITBONE

Symphytum officinale (Boraginaceae)

HISTORY and USES Comfrey's name derives from the Latin *con firma,* i.e. "with strength", from the belief that it could heal broken bones. Comfrey leaves and roots contain *allantoin*, a cell multiplication agent that increases the healing of wounds. Today, it is still highly regarded for its healing properties. Externally it is used for rashes, wounds, and inflammation and skin problems. Internally, comfrey has action over the digestive tract helping to cure ulcers and colitis. It is also used for a variety of respiratory problems.

MAIN PROPERTIES: Digestive problems, anti-inflammatory, wound healing, astringent.

19) CORIANDER

Coriandrum sativum (Umbelliferae)

HISTORY and USES

Coriander use has a medicinal plant has been reported since 1500 B.C. both as a spice and as a medicine. It has now spread well beyond its native Mediterranean and Caucasian regions. It aids in digestion, reduces flatulence and improves appetite. It helps relieving spasms within the gut and counters the effects of nervous tension. Coriander is also chewed to sweeten the breath, especially after consumption of garlic (*Allium sativum*).

It is applied externally as a lotion for rheumatic pain. Coriander essential oil is used in the manufacture of perfumes, cosmetics and dentifrices.

MAIN PROPERTIES: Digestive, antispasmodic, anti-rheumatic.

20) CYMBOPOGON, LEMON GRASS

Cymbopogon citratus (Gramineae)

HISTORY and USES

Native from Sri Lanka and South India, lemon grass is now widely cultivated in the tropical areas of America and Asia. Its oil is used as a culinary flavoring, a scent and medicine. Lemon grass is principally taken as a tea to remedy digestive problems diarrhea and stomach ache. It relaxes the muscles of the stomach and gut, relieves cramping pains and flatulence and is particularly suitable for children. In the Caribbean, lemon grass is primarily regarded as a fever-reducing herb. It is applied externally as a poultice or as diluted essential oil to ease pain and arthritis. MAIN PROPERTIES: Digestive, antispasmodic, analgesic.

21)DAMIANA*Turneradiffusasyn.T.diffusavar.aphrodis iaca*(Turneraceae)
HISTORY and USES
Native from the Gulf of Mexico, damiana has an ancient reputation as an aphrodisiac and is an excellent remedy for the nervous system acting as a stimulant and tonic in cases of mild depression. Damiana has a strongly aromatic, slightly bitter taste. The leaves are used to flavor liqueurs and are taken in Mexico as a substitute for tea.
MAIN PROPERTIES: Nerve tonic, antidepressant, urinary antiseptic.

22) DANDELION
Taraxacum officinale (Compositae)
HISTORY and USES
Occurring naturally in Asia, Dandelion is now a common plant everywhere. Its medicinal virtues were probably introduced in Europe by the Arabs in the 10th Century. Both the Persians and the East Indians used it for liver complaints. Known principally as a weed, dandelion has an astonishing range of health benefits. The leaves, which can be eaten in salads, are a powerful

diuretic. The roots act as a "blood purifier" that helps both kidneys and the liver to remove impurities from the blood. This effect seems to be due to its potassium content. It also acts like a mild laxative and improves appetite and digestion.

MAIN PROPERTIES: Diuretic, digestive, antibiotic, bitter.

23) DILL

Anethum graveolens syn. Peucedanum graveolens (Umbelliferae)

HISTORY and USES

An ancient Egyptian remedy in the Ebers papyrus (c. 1500 BC) recommends dill as one of the ingredients in a pain-killing mixture. The Romans knew dill as anethum, which later became "anise". Dill has always been considered a remedy for the stomach, relieving wind and calming the digestion. Dill's essential oil relieves intestinal spasms and griping and helps to settle colic; hence it is often used in gripe water mixtures. Chewing the seeds improves bad breath. Dill makes a useful addition to cough, cold and flu remedies, and is a mild diuretic. Dill increases milk production, and when taken regularly by nursing mothers, helps to prevent colic in their babies.

MAIN PROPERTIES: Digestive, antibacterial, antispasmodic, diuretic.

24) EUCALYPTUS, BLUE GUM

Eucalyptus globulus (Myrtaceae)

HISTORY and USES

Eucalyptus is native from Australia, where it comprises more than 75% of all trees. A traditional aboriginal remedy, eucalyptus is a powerful antiseptic used all over the world for relieving coughs and colds, sore throats and other infections. The leaves cool the body and relive fever. Inhaling the vapors of the essential oils heated in water, clears sinus and bronchial congestions. *Eucaliptol*, one of the substances found in the essential oil, is one of the main constituents of the many existing commercial formulas of chest rubs for colds. The essential oil has also strong anti-biotic, anti-viral and anti-fungal action. Eucalyptus is a common ingredient in many over-the-counter cold remedies.

MAIN PROPERTIES: Antiseptic, expectorant, stimulates local blood flow, anti-fungal.

25) FENNEL

Foeniculum vulgare (Umbelliferae)

HISTORY and USES

Native to the Mediterranean, fennel has spread to surrou ounding areas, including India. Known to the Greeks and Romans, is was used as food, spice and medicine. The primary use of fennel seeds is to relieve flatulence, but they also settle colic, stimulate the appetite and digestion. Fennel is also diuretic and cxivnti-inflammatory. Like anise (*Pimpinella anisum*) and caraway (*Carum carvi*), it has a calming effect on bronchitis and coughs. An infusion of the seeds may be taken as a gargle for sore throats and as a mild expectorant. Fennel increases breast-milk production and the herb is still used as an eye wash for sore eyes and conjunctivitis. Essential oil from the sweet variety is used for its digestive and relaxing properties.

MAIN PROPERTIES: Digestive, antispasmodic, anti-inflammatory.

26) GARLIC

Allium sativum (Liliaceae)

HISTORY AND USES

Original from Central Asia, garlic is now cultivated worldwide. It was widely known by the ancients, being found in Egyptian tombs and used by Greeks and Romans. Recognized for its pungent odor and taste, garlic is a powerful home medicine for the treatment for a host of health problems. It is one of the most effective anti-biotic plants available, acting on bacteria, viruses and alimentary parasites. It counters many infections, including those of the nose, throat and chest. Garlic is also known to reduce cholesterol, helps circulatory disorders, such as high blood pressure, and lower blood sugar levels, making it useful in cases of late-onset diabetes.

MAIN PROPERTIES: Antibiotic, expectorant, diaphoretic, hypotensive, antispasmodic, expels worms.

27) GINGER

Zingiber officinali (Zingiberaceae)

HISTORY and USES

Ginger is original from Southeast Asia and is now cultivated in most tropical countries. Its citations in ancient texts go back to the 4th century B.C. The Greeks imported it from the East centuries before Discorides recorded its use in the 1st century A.D. Familiar as a spice and flavoring, ginger is also one of the world's best medicines. The Chinese consider ginger as an important drug to treat cold and encourage sweating. Ginger brings relief to digestion, stimulates circulation, reduce headaches and kill intestinal parasites.

MAIN PROPERTIES: Diaphoretic, carminative, circulatory stimulant, inhibits coughing, anti-inflammatory, antiseptic.

28) GINKGO

Ginkgo biloba (Ginkgoaceae)

HISTORY and USES

Ginkgo is thought to be the oldest tree on the planet, first growing about 190 million years ago. It is probably native to China, although there are no wild trees remaining. Though long used as a medicine in its native China, its therapeutic actions have only recently been researched. Traditionally known as an antimicrobial and anti-tubercular action, it has now been shown that ginkgo as a profound activity on brain function and cerebral circulation. This action is useful to prevent dizziness, tinnitus, short-term memory loss, depression and other symptoms related to poor brain circulation. Its effect on poor circulation also used to treat other related disorders like diabetes, hemorrhoids and varicose veins. Ginkgo is also valuable for asthma.

MAIN PROPERTIES: Circulatory stimulant and tonic, anti-asthmatic, antispasmodic, anti-allergenic, anti-inflammatory.

29) GINSENG

Panax ginseng (Araliaceae)

HISTORY and USES

Ginseng is the most famous Chinese herb of all. It is native to north-eastern China, eastern Russia and Korea. The related species *Panax quinquefolious*, occurs in the eastern United States and Canada. Ginseng has ancient and rich history as a medicinal for about 7,000 years. Its value was so great that wars were fought for control of the forests in which it thrived. An Arabian physician brought ginseng back to Europe in the 9th century, yet its ability to improve stamina and resistance to stress became common knowledge in the West only from the 18th century. Ginseng increases mental and physical efficiency and resistance to stress and disease. It often shows a dual response like sedating or
stimulating the central nervous system according to the condition it is being taken to treat. In the West, ginseng is regarded as a life enhancing tonic.

MAIN PROPERTIES: Tonic, stimulant, physical and mental revitalizer.

30) LAVENDER
Lavandula officinalis syn. *L. angustifolia* (Labiatae)
HISTORY AND USES
Lavender is native to the Mediterranean region and is cultivated in France, Spain and elsewhere. It has been used for aromatic purposes by the Romans in washing water and baths. This herb has uses in culinary, cosmetics and medicine. It is effective to cure headaches, especially when related to stress, to clear depression associated with weakness and depression. Externally, lavender oil has been used as a stimulating liniment to help ease aches and pains of rheumatism.
MAIN PROPERTIES: Carminative, relieves muscle spasms, antidepressant, antiseptic and antibacterial, stimulates blood flow.

31) LEMON
Citrus Limon (Rutaceae)
A native from Asia, probably from India, it is now widely cultivated in Italy, California and Australia. Lemon was unknown to the ancient Greeks arriving in Europe probably brought by Roman soldiers returning from Asia Minor. It is one of the most important and versatile natural medicines for home use. A familiar food as well as a remedy, it has a high vitamin C content that helps improve resistance to infection, making it valuable for colds and flu. It is taken as a preventative for many conditions, including stomach infections, circulatory problems and arteriosclerosis. Lemon juice and oil are effective in killing germs. It decreases inflammation and improves digestion.
MAIN PROPERTIES: Antiseptic, anti-rheumatic, antibacterial, antioxidant, reduces fever.

32) MARJORAM,WILD MARJORAM
Origanum vulgare (Labiatae)
HISTORY AND USES

Native from Asia, marjoram is cultivated commercially in several regions. Much used by the ancient Greeks, wild marjoram has had a more significant role in medicine than sweet marjoram (O. majorana). Marjoram tea is an age-old remedy to aid digestion, increase sweating and encourage menstruation. As a steam inhalant, marjoram clears the sinuses and helps relieve laryngitis. Wild marjoram helps settle flatulence and stimulates the flow of bile. Strongly antiseptic, it may be taken to treat respiratory conditions such as coughs, tonsillitis, bronchitis and asthma. The diluted oil can be applied to toothache or painful joints.

MAIN PROPERTIES: Antiseptic, anti-spasmodic, digestive.

33) MELISSA, LEMON BALM
Melissa officinalis (Labiatae)
HISTORY AND USES

Lemon Balm has been cultivated in the Mediterranean region for more than 2,000 years. The Muslim herbalist Avicenna recommended lemon balm for heart problems. Its main action is as a tranquilizer. It calms nervous spasms, colics and hearth spasms. The hot tea promotes sweat that that is good for colds, flus and fevers. Its sedative actions have been used to help in the treatment of psychiatric problems, including dystonia. Lemon's balm anti-histamine action is useful to treat eczema and headaches. Today, this sweet-smelling herb is still widely valued for its calming properties, and new research shows that it can help significantly in the treatment of cold sores.

MAIN PROPERTIES: Relaxant, antispasmodic, increases sweating, carminative, anti-viral, nerve tonic.

34) MOTHERWORT

Leonurus cxixnti-in (Labiatae)

HISTORY AND USES

Native to Europe, motherwort has been used as a medicinal plant in early Greece, where it was used to calm pregnant women suffering from anxiety. The other prominent use of the herb is due to is action over the hearth by decreasing muscle spasms and lowering blood pressure. Other uses include the improvement of fertility, the relief of postpartum depression and menopause.

Antispasmodic and sedative, the herb promotes relaxation rather than drowsiness. However, motherwort stimulates the muscles of the uterus, and is particularly suitable for delayed periods, period pain and premenstrual tension (especially if shock or distress is a factor).

MAIN PROPERTIES: Nervine, emmenagogue, anti-spasmodic, hepatic, hypotensive, cardiac tonic.

35) MYRRH

Commiphora molmol syn. *C. myrrha* (Burseraceae)

HISTORY AND USES

Native to north-east Africa, myrrh is mainly found in Ethiopia, Somalia, Saudi-Arabia, Iran and Thailand. Myrrh has been used in perfumes, incense and embalming. Its astringent, antimicrobial and antiseptic properties have been used to treat acne and boils as well as mild inflammatory conditions. It finds specific use in the treatment of infections in the mouth such as ulcers, cxixnti-infla, phyorrea, as well as catarrhal problems associated with pharyngitis and sinusitis.

MAIN PROPERTIES: Stimulant, antiseptic, anti-inflammatory, astringent, expectorant, antispasmodic, carminative

36) NETTLE
Urtica dioica (Urticaceae)
HISTORY AND USES
Nettle occurs in Eurasia and is naturalized elsewhere, including America and is one of the most applicable plants found. Nettles have supplied fibers for cloth and paper since the Bronze Age into the 20th century. Throughout Europe, it has been used as a spring tonic and general detoxifying remedy. Nettle leaves contain iron and vitamin C, being used for treating anemia and poor circulation. Tea an poultice made from nettle leaves are used to treat eczema and skin conditions. Its astringent properties are used to stop bleeding. Today, nettle is used for hay fever, arthritis, anemia, and, surprisingly, even for nettle rash.
MAIN PROPERTIES: Diuretic, tonic, astringent, prevents hemorrhaging, anti-allergenic, reduces prostate enlargement (root).

37) OLIVE
Olea europaea (Oleaceae)
HISTORY AND USES
The olive was probably first cultivated in Crete in around 3500 BC. The leaves have been used since those times to clean wounds. Olive leaves lower blood pressure and help to improve the function of the circulatory system. They are also mildly diuretic and may be used to treat conditions such as cystitis. Possessing some ability to lower blood sugar levels, the leaves have been taken for diabetes. The oil is nourishing and improves the balance of fats within the blood. It is traditionally taken with lemon juice in

teaspoonful doses to treat gallstones. The oil has a generally protective action on the digestive tract and is useful for dry skin. Externally, it is a good, although sticky, carrier oil for essential oils.

MAIN PROPERTIES: Digestive, diuretic, anti-inflammatory.

38) PARSLEY

Petroselinum crispum (Umbelliferae)

HISTORY AND USES

Parsley is probably native from northern and central Europe and western Asia. It was known in ancient Greece and Rome – but more as a diuretic, digestive tonic and stimulant of the menstrual flow than as a salad herb. Parsley leaves, seed and root treat urinary tract infections and help eliminate kidney stones. It also stimulates appetite and increases blood flow to digestive organs, as well as reduces fevers. Parsley was introduced into Britain in 1548. Parsley has the unusual ability of masking strong odors, that of garlic in particular (which is one of reason for the herb's frequent use as a garnish in cookery). Parsley root is more commonly prescribed than the seeds or leaves in herbal medicine. It is taken as a treatment for flatulence, cystitis and rheumatic conditions. Parsley is also valued as a promoter of menstruation, being helpful both in stimulating a delayed period and in relieving menstrual pain.

MAIN PROPERTIES: Digestive, diuretic.

39) PASSIFLORA, PASSION FLOWER

Passiflora cxxinti-infl (Passifloraceae)

HISTORY AND USES

Passiflora is natural from the north America. Its name comes from its beautiful flowers, thought to represent Christ's crucifixion – 5 stamens for the 5 wounds, 3 styles for the 3 nails and white and purple-blue colors for purity and heaven. The herb has valuable sedative and tranquilizing properties and has a long use as a medicine in Central and North American herbal traditions, being taken in Mexico for insomnia epilepsy and hysteria. The leaves are an ingredient in many pharmaceutical products to treat nervous disorders such as heart palpitations, anxiety, convulsions and sometimes high blood pressure. It is also used to prevent spasms from whooping cough, asthma and other diseases.

MAIN PROPERTIES: Anti-inflammatory, antispasmodic, hypotensive sedative, tranquilizing.

40) PATCHOULI

Pogostemon cablin syn. *P. patchouli* (Labiatae)

HISTORY AND USES

Native to Malaysia and the Philippines, Patchouli is now cultivated in tropical and sub-tropical regions around the world. Patchouli has been used extensively in Asian medicine, appearing in the Chinese, Indian and Arabic traditions. The oil is widely employed as a fragrance and, in India, as an insect repellent. Patchouli is used in herbal medicine in Asia as an aphrodisiac, antidepressant and antiseptic. It is also employed for headaches and fever. Patchouli essential oil is used in aromatherapy to treat skin complaints. It is thought to have a regenerative effect on skin tone and to help clear conditions such as eczema and acne. The oil may also be used for varicose veins and hemorrhoids.

MAIN PROPERTIES: Antiseptic, aromatic, antidepressant.

41) PEPPERMINT

Mentha piperita (Labiatae)

HISTORY AND USES

Peppermint's origin is a mystery, but it has been in existence for a long time – dried leaves were found in Egyptian pyramids dating from around 1000 BC. It was highly valued by the Greeks and Romans, but only became popular in Western Europe in the 18th Century. Peppermint tea helps with indigestion and relaxes the muscles of the digestive tract. Peppermint's chief therapeutic value lies in its ability to relieve wind, flatulence, bloating and colic, though it has many other applications. Studies have shown that it relieves colon spasms and helps to cure ulcers. Peppermint also eases nervous headaches. Menthol, its main constituent, has antibacterial properties. Externally, the essential oil is used in balms and liniments to stimulate hot and cold nerve endings and increase local blood flow.

MAIN PROPERTIES: Carminative, relieves muscle spasms, increases

sweating, stimulates secretion of bile, antiseptic.

42) PEPPER

Piper nigrum (Piperaceae)

HISTORY AND USES

Native to south-western India, pepper is now cultivated in tropical regions around the world. Praised as a spice and a medicine since ancient times, pepper was a vital commodity in world trade for thousands of years. Pepper has a stimulant and antiseptic effect on the digestive tract and the circulatory system. Pepper is commonly taken, either alone or in combination with other herbs and spices, to warm the body, or to improve digestive function in cases of nausea, stomach ache, flatulence, bloating, constipation or lack of appetite. The essential oil eases rheumatic pain and toothache. It is antiseptic and antibacterial, and reduces fever.

MAIN PROPERTIES: Antibacterial, antiseptic, digestive, reduces fever.

43) RADISH *Raphanus sativus* (Cruciferae)
HISTORY AND USES

Radish probably is native from southern Asia. It has been used for medicinal purposes by the Egyptians, Greeks, Romans and Chinese. Radish stimulates the appetite and the digestion. The juice of the black radish is drunk to counter gassy indigestion and constipation. Black radish juice has a tonic and laxative action on the intestines, and indirectly stimulates the flow of bile. Consuming radish generally results in improved digestion, but some people are sensitive to its acridity and strong action. In China, radish is eaten to relieve abdominal distention.

MAIN PROPERTIES: Digestive, mild laxative

44) ROSEMARY
Rosmarinus officinalis (Labiatae)
HISTORY AND USES

Rosemary is native to the Mediterranean region. Rosemary is a well-known and greatly valued herb that is native to southern Europe. It has been used since antiquity to improve and strengthen the memory. Rosemary leaves increase circulation, reduce headaches and have anti-bacterial and fungal properties. Rosemary improves food absorbtion by stimulating digestion, the liver, the intestinal tract, and the gallbladder. It also is used in antiseptic gargles for sore throats, gum problems and canker sores. Rosemary has a long-standing reputation as a tonic, invigorating herb, imparting a zest for life that is to some degree reflected in its distinctive aromatic taste.

MAIN PROPERTIES: Tonic, stimulant, astringent, nervine, cxxivnti inflammatory, carminative.

45) RUE *Ruta graveolens* (Rutaceae)
HISTORY AND USES

Rue is native to Southern Europe. In ancient Greece and Egypt, rue was employed to stimulate menstrual bleeding, to induce abortion and to strengthen the eyesight. The rutin contained in the plant helps to strengthen fragile blood vessels and alleviates varicose veins. Rue is also used due to its antispasmodic properties, especially in the digestive system where it eases griping and bowel tension. The easing of spasms gives it a role in the stopping of spasmodic coughs. In European herbal medicine, rue has also been taken to treat conditions as varied as hysteria, epilepsy, vertigo, colic, intestinal worms, poisoning and eye problems. The latter use is well founded, as an infusion used as an eyewash brings quick relief to strained and tired eyes, and reputedly improves the eyesight.

MAIN PROPERTIES: Antispasmodic, increases peripheral blood circulation, relieves eye tension.

46) SAGE, CLARY CLARY SAGE
Salvia sclarea (Labiatae)
HISTORY AND USES

Clary sage has been perceived both as a weaker version of its close relative, sage (*S. officinalis*), and as a significant herb in its own right. Since the seeds were once commonly used to treat eye problems, it was also known as "clear eye". An antispasmodic and aromatic plant, clary sage is used today mainly to treat digestive problems such as wind and indigestion. It is also regarded as a tonic, calming herb that helps relieve period pain and premenstrual problems. Owing to its estrogen-stimulating action, it is most effective when levels of this hormone are low.

MAIN PROPERTIES: Astringent, antiseptic, aromatic, carminative,
estrogenic, reduces sweating, tonic.

47) SAGE
Salvia officinalis (Labiatae)
HISTORY AND USES
Sage grows from north to central Spain to the west of Balkans and Asia Minor. It was used in Crete in 1600 AD to clear throat well-known cold germ and flu fighter. It has been found to be very effective to reduce many physical emissions like sweating and is an excellent remedy for sore throats, poor digestion and irregular periods. It is also taken as a gently stimulating tonic. It has a slightly warm, noticeably bitter and astringent taste.
MAIN PROPERTIES: Astringent, antiseptic, aromatic, carminative, estrogenic, reduces sweating, tonic.

48) SANDALWOOD
Santalum album (Santalaceae)
HISTORY AND USES
Native to eastern India, sandalwood is cultivated in South-East Asia for the extraction of wood and essential oil. Sandalwood's aroma has been highly esteemed in China and India for thousands of year. The heartwood is most often used in perfumery, but it has also been taken as a remedy in China since around AD 500. Sandalwood and its essential oil are used for their antiseptic properties in treating genito-urinary conditions such as cystitis and gonorrhea. In India, a paste of the wood is used to soothe rashes and itchy skin. In China, sandalwood is held to be useful for chest and abdominal pain.
MAIN PROPERTIES: Antiseptic, aromatic.

49) ST JOHN'S WORT
Hypericum perforatum (Guttiferae)

HISTORY AND USES St. John's wort flowers at the time of the summer solstice, and in medieval Europe it was considered to have powerful magical properties that enabled it to repel evil. The most well-known action of St. John's wort is in repairing nerve damage and reducing pain and inflammation. It is taken to relieve the pain of menstrual cramps, sciatica and arthritis. Th oils is applied to inflammations, sprains, bruises and varicose veins. St. John's wort is also used to treat circulation problems, bronchitis and gout.

MAIN PROPERTIES: Antidepressant, antispasmodic, astringent, sedative, relieves pain, anti-viral.

50) TARRAGON
Artemisia dracunculus (Compositae)

HISTORY AND USES

Tarragon is probably native of southern Europe or the steppes of Asia. Historians believe that tarragon reached Europe brought into Spain by invading Mongols. Tarragon is widely used as a herb in cooking. In French, it is sometimes known as *herbe au dragon*, because of its reputed ability to cure serpent bites. While tarragon stimulates the digestion, it is reputed to be a mild sedative and has been taken to aid sleep. With its mild menstruation-inducing properties, it is taken if periods are delayed. The root has traditionally been applied to aching teeth.

MAIN PROPERTIES: Anti-inflammatory, digestive.

51) TEA TREE
Malaleuca alternifolia (Myrtaceae) Tea tree is native to Australia and is now cultivated extensively. Tea tree, and in particular its essential oil, is one of the most

important natural antiseptics. Useful for stings, burns, wounds and skin infections of all kinds, the herb merits a place in every medicine chest. Its therapeutic properties were first researched during the 1920s and it is now widely used in Europe and the US, as well as in Australia.

MAIN PROPERTIES: Antiseptic, antibacterial, anti-fungal, antiviral.

52) THYME *Thymus vulgaris* (Labiatae)
HISTORY AND USES

Thyme occurs in the west Mediterranean to the southwest Italy. The herb was known to the Sumerians, used by the Egyptians, Greeks and Romans. Thyme was praised by the herbalist Nicholas Culpeper (1616-1654) as "a notable strengthener of the lungs". Its main medicinal application is in treating coughs and clearing congestion. Many current formulas for mouth washes and vapor rubs contain thymol, one of the constituents found in thyme. It also improves digestion, destroys intestinal parasites and is an excellent antiseptic and tonic.

MAIN PROPERTIES: Antiseptic, tonic, relieves muscle spasm, expectorant.

53) TURMERIC
Curcuma longa syn. *C. domestica* (Zingiberaceae)
HISTORY AND USES

Turmeric is native to India and southern Asia where it is extensively cultivated. Best known for its bright yellow color and spicy taste to lovers of Indian food, its medicinal value is not so well known. However, recent research has confirmed the effects traditionally associated in ancient practices in the treatment of digestive and liver problems. The herb has also been shown to inhibit blood-clotting, relieve inflammatory conditions and help lower cholesterol levels.

MAIN PROPERTIES: Stimulates secretion of bile, cxxixnti-inflammatory, eases stomach pain, antioxidant, antibacterial

54) VERBENA
Verbena officinalis (Verbenaceae)
HISTORY AND USES

Native of Europe, verbena is extensively cultivated in other countries. Verbena has long been credited with magical properties and was used in ceremonies by the Romans, Druids of ancient Britain and Gaul. It is a traditional herbal medicine in both China and Europe. Verbena is used in mouth washes for infected gums and as a poultice for hemorrhoids. A tea has been used as a nerve tonic, to treat insomnia and to help digestion. It has tonic, restorative properties, and is used to relieve stress and anxiety, and to improve digestive function.

MAIN PROPERTIES: Nervine, tonic, mild sedative, stimulates bile secretion, mild bitter.

55) WHITE WILLOW
Salix alba (Salicaceae)
HISTORY AND USES

White willow is native to Europe but is also found in North Africa and Asia. White willow is an excellent remedy for arthritic and rheumatic pain, affecting the joints like knees and hips. Famous as the original source of salicylic acid, first isolated in 1838 and synthetically produced in the laboratory in 1899, white willow and closely related species have been used for thousands of years in Europe, Africa, Asia and North America to relieve joint pain and manage fevers. The Greek physician Discorides in the 1st century AD, suggested taking "willow leaves, mashed with a little pepper and drunk with wine" to relieve lower back pain.

MAIN PROPERTIES: Anti-inflammatory, analgesic, reduces fever, anti-rheumatic, astringent.

56) WORMWOOD

Artemisia absinthium (Compositae) HISTORY AND USES Native to Europe, wormwood was called *absintium* by the Romans, what means "bitter". Wormwood leave's primary uses is to stimulate the gallbladder, help prevent and release stones, and to adjust digestive malfunctions. It also increases bile secretion and is useful in expelling intestinal worms. It is taken in small doses and sipped, the intensely bitter taste playing an important part in its therapeutic effect. In the past, wormwood was one of the main flavorings of vermouth (whose name derives from the German for wormwood).

MAIN PROPERTIES: Aromatic bitter, stimulates secretion of bile, anti-inflammatory, eliminates worms, eases stomach pains, mild antidepressant.

57) WILD THYME

Thymus serpyllum (Labiatae)

HISTORY AND USES

Thyme is native to the west Mediterranean to southwest Italy. Like its close relative thyme (*Thymus vulgaris*), wild thyme is strongly antiseptic and anti-fungal. It may be taken as an infusion or syrup to treat flu and colds, sore throats, coughs, whooping cough, chest infections, and bronchitis. Wild thyme has anticatarrhal properties and helps clear a stuffy nose, sinusitis, ear congestion and related complaints. It has been used to expel thread worms and roundworms in children, and is used to settle wind and colic. Wild thyme's antispasmodic action makes it useful and is used to settle wind and colic. Wild thyme is also used in herbal baths and pillows.

MAIN PROPERTIES: Antiseptic, anti-fungal, antispasmodic

58) YLANG –YLANG

Canananga odorata syn. *Canangium odoratum* (Annonaceae)

HISTORY AND USES

Ylang-ylang is native to Indonesia and the Philippines. The flowers are a traditional adornment in the Far East. Their scent is thought to have aphrodisiac qualities. The flowers and essential oil are sedative and antiseptic. The oil has a soothing effect, and its main therapeutic uses are to slow an excessively fast heart rate and to lower blood pressure. With its reputation as an aphrodisiac, ylang-ylang may be helpful in treating impotence.

MAIN PROPERTIES: Antiseptic, aromatic, regulates blood pressure

Thank you for gathering your friends and family to enjoy reading this little book of poetry and the blessings of entertainment and enlightenment of this Halloween season. Be Blessed with love, good health, happiness and prosperity.

God is always with us and his love never fails.

Jackie Spencer

2013